## BASIC RULES OF THE GAME

Baseball is played with a bat and a ball, and two teams of nine players each. One team takes a turn at bat while the other plays the field. The teams switch places after the team that is up at bat gets three outs. When both teams have taken a turn at bat, it's called an inning. Standard games have nine innings, but youth games may have fewer. Nick's league plays six innings.

To score, a batter must touch each base, in order, and then home plate. The team that scores the most runs wins the game. A game never ends in a tie. Extra innings will be played until one team wins.

Youth league rules may differ somewhat from major league rules.

# NICK PLAYS
# Baseball

## RACHEL ISADORA

G. P. Putnam's Sons • New York

This is Nick.
He loves baseball.

*For Nick, who loves baseball*

Published simultaneously in Canada. Printed in Hong Kong by South China Printing Co. (1988) Ltd.
Designed by Donna Mark and Semadar Megged. Text set in Trump Mediaeval.
The art was done in watercolor on Strathmore 500 Bristol.
Library of Congress Cataloging-in-Publication Data
Isadora, Rachel.    Nick plays baseball / Rachel Isadora.    p. cm.
Summary: Uses the story of Nick and his teammates' championship baseball game to provide
an introduction to aspects of the game of baseball including equipment, player positions, and rules.
1. Baseball—Juvenile literature. [1. Baseball.] I. Title.   GV867.5 .I82 2001   796.357—dc21   00-038228
ISBN 0-399-23231-1
10  9  8  7  6  5  4  3  2  1
FIRST IMPRESSION

Nick has practice every week for two hours during baseball season. The championship game is coming up this Saturday. Nick's mom drops him off at the baseball field. Coach Brian comes over to greet him. "Hey, Nick, why don't you do some warm-ups, and then we're going to have drills."

205 Ft.

# WARMING UP

The players run bases to
build up speed and stamina.

They practice their fielding skills and
throw ground balls to each other.

Coach Brian says that practice is just as important as the games. "At practice you improve your skills and learn to work together as a team."

Nick wishes he had practice every day instead of every week.

Coach Brian hits pop flies to each player. When a player from the opposing team catches a pop fly in a game, the batter will be called out.

# BATTING DRILLS

Learning to hit takes years of practice. Being a good hitter requires the right stance, the right timing, strength and a good eye.

Mady is choking up too much on the bat. Coach Brian tells her to lower her grip.

Max practices stepping into the ball.

Nick works on his swing with Coach Brian.

Charlie is learning how to bunt. To bunt, a player taps the ball and surprises the opposing team. A bunt is used to allow the batter enough time to get to first base safely. A sacrifice bunt is used to advance a runner to another base.

# PITCHING DRILLS

Coach Brian has Nick, Olivia, Danny and Jose practice their pitching. Nick is the best pitcher on his team. He's got a strong arm and great aim.

In youth leagues, pitchers are often allowed to pitch only a certain number of innings, so every team needs backup pitchers.

Olivia has a good windup, but she needs to keep her eye on the hitter.

Danny knows to take his time and concentrate.

Jose needs to control his pitch. He's strong, but often throws wild pitches that get by the catcher.

Nick throws a good fastball, but sometimes he surprises the hitter and pitches slow.

Even when he's at home, Nick practices pitching, hitting and sliding. Someday he hopes to be on a professional team. During the season, Nick goes with his family to watch the major leagues play.

pitcher

runner sliding into second base

left-handed batter

right-handed batter

Finally, it's the day of the championship game. Nick unpacks his bag after he arrives at the field.

sport bag

baseball: has a cork core which is wrapped with string and then covered in leather.

cap: protects the player's face and eyes from the sun

team shirt

pants

"Did you bring your good-luck glove?" Ben asks.
"I never forget it," Nick says and throws a ball to Ben.

cleats: give players better traction on the field

stirrups: match the team colors

# Equipment

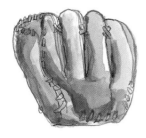

baseball glove: made of leather. Should be flexible and comfortable and feel as if it were made just for you.

catcher's mitt

batting gloves: help prevent blisters. They allow you to have a firmer grip on the bat.

bats: made from either wood or aluminum. They are different lengths and weights. The lighter the bat, the easier it is to swing. Choose a bat that you can control. Sometimes batting tape is used for a better grip.

batting helmet          catcher's helmet

helmet: made of plastic; protects the head and face.

donut: placed on a bat for extra weight. Just before players go up to bat, they sometimes use a donut while taking practice swings "on deck." When the donut is taken off, the bat feels lighter and the player can swing faster.

catcher's gear: well-padded, provides extra protection.

cup and athletic supporter: boys wear these for protection

When the field is ready, the two teams go to their dugouts.
The Rockets huddle around Coach Brian.

"Remember, always keep your eye on the ball," he tells them.
"We are a great team. Do your best and HAVE FUN!"

# COACH BRIAN'S TIPS

The quickest way to reach second base, third base and home plate is to slide. Keep your hands up. Slide on your bottom. Try to keep your foot up to avoid injury.

To catch a grounder, bend your body over the ball. Field the ball quickly into the glove using two hands.

You can use your glove to block the sun and protect your face. Squeeze the ball with your glove to secure it. With a fly ball, catch it above your head with both hands.

Remember, first base is the only base you can overrun and not be tagged out.

Coach Brian assigns the positions and gives the players the batting order.

Nick is the pitcher and will be fourth at bat.

The Rockets are the home team, so the Clippers are at bat first.

Nick gets a few practice throws to Danny, the catcher. "Let's play ball!" the umpire shouts.

Once the batting order is given to the umpire, it cannot be changed. Substitutes can be used, but once a player is removed, he or she cannot return to the game. The umpire makes certain everyone obeys the rules.

"Play ball!"

umpire

Center field

2.05 Ft.

Right field

Second base

First base

Foul line

Clippers Coach

The first batter steps up to the plate.
Nick looks at his height to find his strike zone.
The batter swings.
"Strike one!" the umpire calls.
Nick throws a ball then two more strikes.

Nick takes his time and carries through on his pitch.

Gripping the ball: the pitcher uses different grips to give the ball spin, make it travel in a straight or curved path or change its speed in the air. These two are the most common pitches in youth leagues.

Four-seam fastball: grip the ball across the seams.

Two-seam fastball: grip the ball along the direction of the seams.

"Out!" the umpire calls.

Nick strikes out the next batter, too.

The third batter gets a hit and runs to first base, just in time.

"Safe!" the umpire shouts.

The strike zone, shown by the red balls, is above the plate from your chest to your knees. If you do not swing at a pitch in the strike zone or swing at a pitch and miss, the umpire calls a strike. After three strikes, the batter is called out. A ball is called when a pitch is outside the strike zone (shown by the blue balls) and the batter does not swing at it. When the umpire calls four balls, the batter walks to first base.

The fourth batter hits two foul balls and then a fly ball.
Ben catches it in left field.
Three outs.
The Rockets are up.

"I've got it!"

When a player hits a ball and
it goes outside the foul lines,
it is called a foul ball. Whenever
a player hits a foul ball, it counts
as a strike, unless the player already
has two strikes. Then the player can
continue to hit foul balls until he or
she strikes out or hits a fair ball.

At the bottom of the fifth inning, the score is Clippers 2, Rockets 0.

| | 1 | 2 | 3 | 4 | 5 | 6 | 7 | 8 |
|---|---|---|---|---|---|---|---|---|
| Rockets | 0 | 0 | 0 | 0 | | | | |
| Visitor | 0 | 1 | 0 | 1 | 0 | | | |

When Mady, the third batter, goes up to bat, Nick is on deck. He puts a donut on his bat and takes some practice swings.

Mady hits a line drive and gets a double.

Now, Nick's up. "Strike one!" the umpire calls. Nick steps away from the plate. He takes a practice swing and a deep breath.

Then, he steps back to the plate. "Keep your eye on the ball," he says to himself. The pitcher winds up and throws.

Nick swings.
*POW!*
But he's out on a pop fly.
"Strong hit, but a little late," Coach Brian tells Nick.

An hour and a half into the game, Coach Brian reminds the players to stay alert. The Rockets take the field at the bottom of the sixth inning.

Be ready to run. After the ball crosses the plate, a runner can steal bases.

Be ready to catch the ball.

Be ready to field the ball. Be ready to react as soon as it is hit.

# MORE TIPS FROM COACH BRIAN

Don't be distracted by airplanes flying overhead!

Don't pick flowers in the outfield!

Don't run with untied shoelaces. Call time out so the umpire will stop the game.

The Rockets cheer on their teammates as they go up to bat.
"Don't forget to put on a helmet!" Olivia calls to Ben.
There are a lot of rules the players must follow. Wearing
a helmet at bat is one of the most important safety rules.

Do not throw the bat or
you can be called out.

# RULES TO ABIDE BY

Be a team player.

Batters and runners must wear head protection.

Boys must also wear cups.

When you run from home plate to first base, you must run between the foul line and the line parallel to it or you will be called out.

Never argue with the umpire.

Most coaches don't allow their players to eat during the game. Having a drink is fine.

Don't block a player when he or she is running.

The pitcher must be in contact with the rubber mound when she or he begins delivery.

If the batter hits the ball when you are on first base, you have to run. This is called a forced run.

Make certain your baseball shirt is tucked in and your cap has the brim in front.

"I've got it!"

Call for the ball when you run to catch it. This will help you avoid a collision with a teammate.

The score is tied, 2–2.
Mady hits a single and runs to first base.

Then, Nick is up.

He hits a line drive, past the shortstop, through the gap.

The ball rolls all the way to the fence.

Mady runs home.

"Rockets win!" the umpire calls. "Rockets win!"
Everyone jumps up and down.
"What a game!" Coach Brian yells.

Both teams line up.
They shake hands as they pass each other.
"Great game," a player from the Clippers says to Nick.
"You've got a super team!" Nick smiles.
The teams return to their dugouts.
There are sandwiches, drinks and lots of snacks.
"Now, you can eat," Coach Brian says, laughing.

The Rockets pose for
a team photograph.

When Nick returns home, he changes out of his muddy
uniform. His mom asks if he wants something to eat.
  But Nick quickly unpacks his bag and takes out his bat
and glove...

and runs outside to play ball with his neighbors.

# The Rockets

...lie
...eld

Ben
shortstop

Jose
second base

Olivia
center field